Welcome to
STARVATION LAKE

by Gloria Whelan
illustrated by Lynne Cravath

A STEPPING STONE BOOK™

Random House 🏠 New York

For Trevor and Greyson
—G.W.

To Sigi
—L.C.

www.randomhouse.com/kids

Library of Congress Cataloging-in-Publication Data
Whelan, Gloria.
Welcome to Starvation Lake / by Gloria Whelan ; illustrated by
Lynne Cravath. — 1st Random House ed.
     p.   cm.
"A Stepping Stone book."
SUMMARY: When a tire fire causes a punk rock band to take a detour
to Starvation Lake, the fourth-grade students talk them into playing
at the school fund-raiser.
ISBN 0-307-26506-4 (pbk.) — ISBN 0-307-46506-3 (lib. bdg.)
[1. Schools—Fiction. 2. Rock music—Fiction.]   I. Cravath, Lynne Woodcock, ill.
II. Title.   PZ7.W5718Wg 2003   [Fic]—dc21   2003000719

Printed in the United States of America 12 11 10 9 8 7 6 5 4 3
First Random House Edition

Contents

1
The Usual Snowstorm

It was another perfectly awful day in Starvation Lake. The town was lost in a swirl of snow. Except for the snowplow, the streets were deserted, but the single traffic light continued to blink red and green.

Outside town, the lake was a white circle of ice. It was frozen six months of the year. Even when it finally thawed, it wasn't much of a lake. In a dry year, it was a swamp. In a rainy year, the only fish anyone could catch were blue gills, which didn't need a lot of water to thrash around in.

The Starvation Lake Elementary School

bus lumbered through the snow. Theresa was the first passenger to get on. "Hi, Elvera," she said to the bus driver.

Elvera didn't bother with her usual greeting. She was concentrating on the layer of ice on Highway 73.

A county truck passed the bus, spitting sand onto the slick road. It just so happened that Elvera's husband was driving the truck.

He lowered his window and called out, "How's it going, Elvera?"

Elvera opened her window and answered, "How's it going, Wilks?"

Theresa brushed the snow off her coat. She flung herself into the best seat on the bus—the one nearest the heater. As usual, Theresa spent the trip to school writing another chapter of her novel. So far she had fifty-three chapters. She was so busy with chapter fifty-four, she hardly noticed the other students climbing onto the bus.

Theresa's novel was about a girl named Amber. Amber had moved to California from a state where it snowed all the time. She'd left all her winter clothes behind. Today she was going shopping. Theresa was trying to decide if Amber should buy a bikini or a one-piece bathing suit.

Theresa's best friend, Stacey, dropped down next to her. Like Theresa, Stacey was dressed in a ski parka and torn jeans with peeks of long underwear underneath. But Stacey also had on a straw hat.

Theresa looked up from her notebook and stared at Stacey's hat. "In case you haven't noticed, it's winter," she pointed out.

"Weird Mom came down to breakfast

in shorts," Stacey explained. "She said if we started wearing our summer clothes maybe spring would hurry up."

"Your mom is bizarre," Theresa said.

Theresa secretly wished her own mom was a little more weird. Her mother was the animal rescue officer. She was very softhearted. The family always had a lot of dogs around.

"Tell me about it," Stacey said. Absent-mindedly, she brushed dog hair off Theresa's parka. "What's Amber doing today?" Stacey asked, looking down at Theresa's notebook.

"Shopping for a bathing suit," Theresa said. She scraped a little peephole in the frosted bus window.

Theresa and Stacey looked out at the snow squalls and sighed.

Stacey said, "At least you can *imagine* you're in California while you're making your story up." She grinned at Theresa. "When you finish your novel, you can put it in the school library. Then we'll have *two* books."

Theresa kicked at her book bag. Stacey was exaggerating about the library—but not much.

"I don't know why I bother to take these books home," Theresa said. "I've read every one ten times. The school never has any money left over for new books in the library. Especially now that we're buying computers."

"Do you think anyone will come to the fund-raiser tomorrow night?" Stacey asked. The fourth grade was putting on a talent show to buy books for the library.

"Our folks will come. And some of the teachers." With a big sigh, Theresa added, "No one else will." She thought of all those empty spaces on the library shelves.

The bus slid to a stop at the Mallows' turkey farm. Marvin climbed onboard, shaking off snow and turkey feathers. Theresa and Stacey stopped talking to stare at him. He had blue eyes, long eyelashes, and blonde hair that curled around his shoulders. Theresa longed to reach up and pluck the turkey feathers from his curls.

Then she noticed Marvin was clutching a new CD of the Putrid Armpits, her favorite group.

"Can I see it?" she asked eagerly.

He handed the CD to her. "I heard the Armpits are playing in Desolation

tonight." Desolation, the nearest large town, was about fifty miles away.

"I'd give anything to go." Theresa admired the picture on the CD, featuring four men in black leather with lots of earrings, tattoos, and spiky purple hair.

"Me, too, but it's too far and too much money," Stacey said.

The bus pulled up in front of the Faith Friendship Community Reformed Church, and Bethany Conway got on. Her father was the pastor of Faith Friendship.

Theresa asked Bethany, "Did you write one yesterday?"

Bethany wrote a poem every day of her life. Theresa and Bethany had agreed they were both going to be famous authors. They planned to live in New York City and be driven around in limos.

"Yes. You want to hear it?" Bethany asked. Without waiting for an answer, she began reciting.

Snowfall

In the morning
At first light
A beautiful sight
Snow, fluffy and loose
Like the down of a goose,
Falls on the rabbit all dead
And the snow turns red.

"Ugh!" Stacey said. "Why do your poems have such unhappy endings?"

"Poets are supposed to be unhappy," Bethany said with a cheerful smile.

A few minutes later the bus pulled into

the driveway of the Starvation Lake elementary school. The snowbanks in the parking lot were so high, Theresa could hardly see the school. She gave one last wistful thought to California and followed the other students off the bus.

2
The Tire Fire

Theresa, Stacey, Bethany, and Marvin hurried toward Ms. LaForest's room. This morning, Ms. LaForest looked great in her pink and green jumper with a watermelon pink turtleneck and lime green tights. Theresa thought Ms. LaForest was the best-dressed teacher in school.

Theresa settled into her seat. The principal's voice was already booming over the loudspeaker.

"Good morning, ladies and gentlemen," Mr. Chickering said. "Today is Thursday, March 6th. The temperature is fifteen degrees. Lunch today will be *jambon* with sweet potato *purée, crudités,* and lemon *gâteau.*"

The cook in charge of the cafeteria had started taking gourmet cooking lessons. Ms. LaForest kept a French dictionary in class just for the morning menu. She checked it now and whispered to the class, "Ham with mashed sweet potatoes, celery and carrot sticks, and lemon cake." Theresa breathed a sigh of relief.

The principal signed off with *The Pledge of Allegiance.*

"Now, boys and girls," Ms. LaForest announced, "it's time to check where the Iditarod racers are today." The fourth-grade class was following the Alaskan dogsled race on the internet.

Ms. LaForest went slowly over to the class computer. Theresa saw that her hands were shaking. Computers made Ms. LaForest nervous. Trying to get on the internet terrified her.

"Looks like we need Tommy again," Theresa whispered to Stacey.

Tommy Kewaysaw was already on his way to help out. He was wearing a Sign of the Wolf Indian Casino T-shirt. Tommy's mother worked in the casino office. Tommy used the computer there all the time.

He logged on for Ms. LaForest. "The Iditarod racers are halfway between Anchorage and Nome," he told the class.

In no time, the class was sticking little colored pins in the map of Alaska. The pins marked how far the dogsleds had traveled.

Just as Ms. LaForest began to relax, the

loudspeaker rumbled. That was a sign that Mr. Chickering was going to make an announcement. His voice sounded frantic. And a little muffled.

Theresa smiled at Stacey. They both knew this time of day Mr. Chickering would be scarfing down a doughnut.

"Attention, ladies and gentlemen and faculty. We have an emergency. The sheriff has just notified me that there is a fire at Fred's Tire Salvage. Because of the toxic fumes, families close to the fire are being evacuated to our school. Also Highway 73 on the other side of Starvation Lake has been closed due to poor visibility from the smoke. Motorists will be sent here."

Then Mr. Chickering's voice took on a soldierlike sound. Theresa could almost hear marching music in the background.

"I expect every Starvation Lake student to rise to the occasion."

The entire fourth grade raced to the window.

"Students, remain in your seats!" Ms. LaForest ordered.

"But Mr. Chickering *said* we should rise!" Kevin Brown said. Both of Kevin's parents were lawyers. Kevin never missed a chance to argue.

The whole class knew about Fred's Tire Salvage yard. Ever since it had opened, people had complained that it was an eyesore. But no one ever dreamed the hundreds of tires would go up in flames.

"Look at the clouds of black smoke!" Theresa said.

Mr. Chickering was still talking in a take-charge voice. "We will be using the gym for our visitors. I want you to make them feel at home here at Starvation Lake Elementary. And now for *The Pledge of*...No, no. We did that earlier." Mr. Chickering's voice faded away.

Everyone was staring out the window. Bethany said, "Theresa! There's your Dad!"

Theresa looked where Bethany was pointing. Her father was escorting a row of cars into the school parking lot. He was the Sheriff of Desolation County.

Mothers and small children who lived near the fire were hurried into the school. Several cars pulled up and men and women in business suits got out. They were hanging onto their briefcases as tightly as the mothers were holding onto their babies.

A huge truck pulled into the parking lot. "Wow!" Marvin said. "That's an eighteen wheeler." A couple climbed out and headed for the school.

Theresa watched four men stumble out of a van. The men looked around and shook their heads at where they found themselves. They were dressed alike in heavy wool sweaters.

"I've seen those four guys before," Marvin said in a puzzled voice.

"They sure don't live around here," Theresa said. "Where could you have run into them?"

She looked at Marvin for an answer.

"I don't know," he said. "I only know their faces are familiar." He stared at the four men. "And it wasn't too long ago," he insisted.

3
Surprise Guests

The class didn't do much work on the Iditarod after that. Students kept rushing over to the window to look at the swirling black smoke. Ms. LaForest held up two fingers, which was a serious signal for everyone to be quiet, but no one was looking at her.

Theresa asked for a bathroom pass. Then everyone else did, too. The whole class wanted to walk by the gym where the people were gathered.

Ms. LaForest kept saying, "You can't *all* have to go!" But Theresa knew she wouldn't dare say no.

Trying desperately to get their attention, Ms. LaForest announced, "We're going to use the tire fire to learn a little geography."

She sent Tommy up to the world map to show where the rubber for tires came from. He pointed out Africa and India with no trouble.

Theresa stood at the map a long time trying to find Sri Lanka and Malaysia. When she got back to her seat, she whispered to Stacey, "Some countries get themselves hidden away in really dumb places."

Ms. LaForest explained, "Tires are made of fake rubber as well as real rubber. Rubber is composed of hydrocarbon." The students' eyes started to glaze over.

Ms. LaForest gave up. She switched to the Native American unit. It was the class's favorite. But today no one listened to Stacey's report on Sitting Bull. No one listened to Theresa's paper on "The Fate of the Buffalo." And Theresa thought it was really good, too.

Finally Tommy helped Ms. LaForest out as he always did. "I can teach the class how to do our tribal dance," he offered. "It's the dance we do every year for the Desolation County Powwow."

Theresa perked up. That sounded much better than Malaysian rubber. The students provided drum music by slapping the tops of their desks. Even Ms. LaForest got carried away, keeping time with her lime green, fake lizard pumps. They were all making so much noise they didn't see the principal, Mr. Chickering, enter the classroom.

Ms. LaForest hastily held up the two-finger silence signal. She explained that the dance was part of their classwork.

The principal waved away her explanation. "Things are getting a little out of control in the gym. I'm asking the fourth graders to give us a hand," Mr. Chickering said. "Are there volunteers?"

Theresa's hand shot up. So did twenty-seven others. It meant getting out of class. Ms. LaForest picked six students, including Theresa.

The volunteers practically ran to the gym. Mr. Chickering was right. Things in the gym were crazy. Theresa saw the four men in wool sweaters arguing with her dad.

"We've got a gig tonight. We have to get out of here," the men insisted.

The couple from the truck said, "We're due in Minnesota tomorrow morning."

The men and women hugging their briefcases looked unhappy.

"I have to be in Ohio this evening," said one of them.

"I have an important deal in the works," said another.

Sheriff Bloncheck only shook his head. "No one leaves until the fire department gets the smoke cleared away. You can't see a foot ahead of you on the road."

Theresa was proud of the firm way her father was handling everyone. She recognized his authoritative voice. It was the same one he used at home when he ordered the dogs to stop raiding the food from their dinner table.

But the loud complaints didn't stop.

And the angry voices were making the babies cry. Their wailing got louder and louder. Theresa decided to be firm like her father. She turned to the briefcase people and held up two fingers, explaining that it was the signal to quiet down. They just looked at her.

Tommy cleared his throat. "Our school has computers with modems. You can check your E-mail," he told them. One after another, the briefcase people gratefully followed Tommy out of the gym.

Kevin rounded up the little kids. Stacey got some crayons and paper for them. Theresa and Bethany went to help Mary, the cook, in the lunchroom kitchen.

Mary was wearing her new, high, white chef's hat. The trouble was, the hat kept getting knocked off. Mary always forgot to bend over when she went through the kitchen door. Theresa picked it up for the third time and handed it back to her.

"I'm a little nervous," Mary said. "I don't know about this. I've never cooked for anyone outside the school before. Who knows what fancy restaurants some of these business people are used to? And there isn't nearly enough food to go around."

"We'll just have to pretend it's loaves and fishes," Bethany said. She picked up a lot of that stuff from her father, Reverend Conway.

Tommy was back from helping the briefcase people. "There's plenty of sweet potatoes so you ought to put those first in the line," he suggested. "People take a lot of what's first." Tommy's father was the chef at the Sign of the Wolf Indian Casino.

"I know!" Theresa had a great idea. "I'll tell them in the office to call around town for food." She headed for the office, happy to be helping out.

By lunchtime, Theresa was thrilled to see the kitchen overflowing. Tommy's dad sent over a big pan of corn pudding from the casino. The Hole in the Wall café in town sent five super-size pizzas. The Mallows sent a roast turkey from their farm. Bethany's mother contributed three angel food cakes she had baked for the church's potluck supper.

Theresa peeked under the aluminum foil covering a glass pan. "What's that?" she asked. It was sort of a sickly green and stringy, and it smelled.

Stacey said, "Weird Mom brought a

casserole of artichokes, sauerkraut, and tofu she made." Stacey gave Theresa a smile. "At least now I won't have to eat it for supper."

Theresa watched Mr. Chickering trying to make up his mind between turkey and pizza. He chose both.

By this time, Theresa felt a little hungry herself. She filled her own plate and wandered over to a table where Marvin was sitting with the four men, the couple from the truck, and a briefcase man.

The truck couple pulled up a chair for Theresa and introduced themselves. "We're Jean and Jim Sims."

Jean was nearly as tall as Jim. They both wore their hair pulled back in ponytails. They had on matching T-shirts that said, "Give us a call and we'll haul."

Theresa, who had never been outside Desolation County, sighed. "I guess you have been all over," she said.

"Every state in the union," answered Jim.

"Except Hawaii. We're waitin' until they build a bridge." Jean grinned.

"Have you ever been to California?" Theresa asked. Just saying the name out loud was exciting.

"Lots of times," Jim told her. "Why?"

"I'd give anything to see what it's like." Theresa needed to know if California was really the way she described it in her novel. She hoped it was.

"We could send you some postcards from there," Jean offered.

"Would you really? That would be terrific." Theresa had never imagined when she got up this morning that she would actually be meeting people who had been to California.

"It'll be fun for us, too. We don't have any family to send postcards to. Will you write back?" Jim asked.

"I'll get the whole class to write," Theresa promised.

She overheard the briefcase man say to the men in sweaters, "I didn't know a town named Starvation Lake existed. Starvation's the perfect name for this town."

One of the four men spoke up. "I think the town has treated us pretty well. And I'm definitely not starving. That lunch was better than anything we've had in a long time," he said.

"Yep," said Jean. "I think I'll get some more."

Jim followed Jean to the cafeteria line.

"What do you four guys do?" the brief-case man asked.

"We have a little band," one of the four said.

"Local group?"

"Not exactly."

"Like the Beach Boys?"

"Not exactly."

Marvin had been staring at the four men. Suddenly he shot up from his seat. "It's you! You're them! Lorn and Tech and Spike and Mitch. It's the Putrid Armpits!"

4
Stars in Starvation

"The Putrid Armpits?" Theresa stared at the four guys. They didn't look like their CD covers.

"You look so different. Where's your black leather?" Marvin asked.

"And your earrings?" Theresa wanted to know.

Marvin was puzzled. "Where are your tattoos?"

"Your hair isn't purple either," Theresa said. She was more and more confused.

"We only wear leather on the stage. It sticks to chairs and won't bend much when you sit down. Hot, too," Lorn said.

"Those tattoos," Spike explained, "we get them out of cereal boxes. Slap 'em on and wash 'em off."

"Our purple hair comes out of a spray bottle," Mitch said. "I can't always look like I do on the albums. I've got to turn up for my kids' school plays and Little League games."

"You've got kids!" Theresa was amazed.

"Sure. We're all married with families. We're just four guys who enjoy making music together."

Marvin looked worshipfully at the Armpits. "I have every one of your albums. I listen to them every day."

"Don't you have something better to do with your time?" Mitch smiled at him. "Maybe you ought to be doing your homework or reading a book."

"There aren't a lot of books around," Theresa confessed.

"What about your school library?" Lorn wanted to know.

"The school doesn't have enough money to buy books," Marvin said.

Theresa told them, "Our class is going to have a talent show tomorrow night to raise money for books." She shook her head sadly. "No one except our parents will come."

"Why not?" Tech asked.

"We're just doing an amateur night and selling cocoa and cookies," Theresa explained. "People around here would rather stay home and watch TV. Last time we had a show, we only raised $2.23. It wasn't enough for one book." Theresa couldn't help looking discouraged.

Lorn said, "I'll tell you what. How would it be if we turned up for the fund-raiser? We could announce it tonight at our performance in Desolation. I mean— we wouldn't want to steal the spotlight from you. We'd just come on afterward. Sort of finish the show." Lorn looked at the other Armpits. They nodded their agreement.

"We could never afford you," Marvin said.

Spike laughed. "No problem. We won't charge anything."

Theresa could hardly believe what she was hearing. "Do you mean it?" she asked.

"Just tell us what time to turn up," Tech said.

"There's just one thing." Marvin was thinking about what his parents had said when they saw the cover of his CD. "Could you skip the black leather and the purple hair and all the rest?"

"Sure. It'll save us time," Mitch said. "Anyway my wife complains about that purple stuff getting on my shirt collars."

Theresa and Marvin raced to tell the other fourth-grade volunteers. It was hard to make them believe that the Armpits would actually perform at the school. When they were finally convinced, they danced around singing the Armpits' big hit, "Don't Throw Up When I Say I Love You."

Kevin interrupted them. "To make it legal, we'll have to get Mr. Chickering's OK." They hurried over to the principal.

Mr. Chickering looked at the four young men in their sweaters and neatly

pressed pants. "Sure. I'd be glad to have them perform at amateur night. Do they have a name for their group?" Mr. Chickering asked.

Theresa started to say, "The Pu—" but Kevin kicked her.

"We didn't ask their name," Kevin said. Which Theresa had to admit was true.

"It's all set," Kevin told the Armpits.

"Could you get here around seven?" Theresa asked.

"We'll be here," Lorn promised.

A briefcase man stood up and called out to get everyone's attention.

"On behalf of all of us who have enjoyed your hospitality, we would like to thank you. I overheard some of the kids talking about a fund-raiser for books. To show our thanks, we want to make a donation of fifty dollars to your library."

There was an enthusiastic round of applause. Theresa clapped the hardest. For the first time that day, the briefcase people smiled. They smiled even more when Sheriff Bloncheck walked through the door and announced, "The road is now open, everyone. The fire is under control."

Theresa called to Jim and Jean, "Don't forget the postcard."

The Armpits waved good-bye. "See you guys tomorrow night!"

"Do you think they'll really come?" Theresa asked Marvin. She tried to imagine the library shelves filled with books instead of dust balls.

Marvin sounded doubtful. "I read somewhere they get thousands of dollars for a performance."

"They promised," Bethany said. She couldn't imagine anyone promising something and then not doing it. That would be almost like a sin.

"With the Putrid Armpits in the show, we'll have to work hard on our own acts," Stacey reminded them.

Everyone went quiet. They hadn't rehearsed and the show was only one day away.

"Let's go ask Ms. LaForest if we can practice instead of doing our history unit," Theresa said. It wasn't as if they were studying anything important. It was just the history of Desolation County.

Ms. LaForest shook her head. "You've already lost most of the day," she told them.

"But this terrific group is going to be

here," Kevin pleaded. "They'll be watching us. And we stink."

"Don't use the word 'stink,' Kevin," Ms. LaForest said. "Remember our class motto, 'We are all special in a special way.' It's very nice of that group to come and sing. Maybe they do folk songs like 'On Top of Old Smoky.'"

"I don't think so, Ms. LaForest," said Theresa. "But you're right. They're really special in their own special way. You'll see tomorrow night."

No one looked at anyone else for fear they'd burst out laughing.

5
Mr. Chickering Says No

That night, Theresa was listening to the radio to be sure there wouldn't be a blizzard for the talent show. She was startled to hear the WDSL announcer say the Putrid Armpits would be appearing at Starvation Lake Elementary School.

After that, things went to pieces.

In the morning, Mr. Chickering had so many calls from parents objecting to the Armpits that he forgot to make his usual announcements. All the students were left facing the flag.

Finally he gasped out *The Pledge of Allegiance* and said, "Just look at the calendar for the date, out the window for the weather, and eat whatever Mary's dishing up. Also, I want to see the fourth-grade volunteers down here in my office *immediately.*"

Ms. LaForest, in beige slacks and a matching sweater, looked like she was going to cry. She sent them on their way.

Theresa felt awful as she trudged down the hall. In her mind, she saw all the new books flying off the library shelves.

Mr. Chickering put down his doughnut and wiped the powdered sugar from his mouth. Theresa winced as he glared down at them. "You told me you didn't know the group's name!" he thundered.

Since his parents were lawyers, Kevin was always careful about wording things exactly. Now he corrected Mr. Chickering.

"I believe we said we didn't 'ask' their name, sir."

"Don't quibble-quabble with me, Kevin Brown. I'm ordering you kids to get hold of that motley group and tell them to stay away from here."

"But Mr. Chickering," Theresa pleaded, "we're desperate for library books. And they've already announced on the radio that the Armpits are going to be at our school. If everybody comes and the Armpits aren't here, there might be a riot or something."

Theresa really didn't believe that. But after writing a chapter of a novel every day, it was easy to imagine almost anything happening.

Mr. Chickering shook his head. "Impossible. Marvin's parents brought in one of their albums. Black leather, earrings, purple hair, tattoos! Not in this school!"

"But they promised they wouldn't wear those things. You saw them in the gym. Their pants were *pressed*. That's how they'll look at the talent show," Marvin said.

"What kind of songs would they sing?" Mr. Chickering asked. Theresa could see from the way he reached for the rest of his doughnut that he was weakening.

"Hymns," Bethany said. Theresa stared at her, her mouth open. Bethany never lied. But her face wasn't even red.

"Well, all right," Mr. Chickering said reluctantly. "But one purple hair or one inch of black leather and out they go! Now, whose mother is making the cookies tonight? Not your mother, Stacey?" Mr.

Chickering asked. The last cookies Weird Mom had brought were made from pumpkin seeds and oat bran.

"No, sir," Stacey said. "Bethany's mom is bringing the cookies."

"Chocolate chip and peanut butter," Bethany promised.

Mr. Chickering smiled for the first time that morning. "Very nice, Bethany."

But Theresa wasn't thinking about cookies. She was thinking about the Putrid Armpits. They were going to perform for the library fund-raiser right in Starvation Lake Elementary School!

6
The No-show Talent Show

The school parking lot was filled long before the talent show began. People streamed through the doors, shaking and stamping away snow.

Theresa and Marvin sat at a table by the entrance to the gym, taking in the money. Admission was a dollar a person. Kids under twelve got in free by bringing a used paperback for the library.

"Gosh, look at how the dollar bills are piling up." To Theresa they looked like green books. "People must be coming from all over to hear the Putrid Armpits."

"Admission last night in Desolation was

twenty dollars," Marvin reminded her. "These people are getting a bargain."

Theresa noticed that some members of the school board and the Parents and Teachers Organization looked seriously angry. They still paid their dollar.

"We're in big trouble," Theresa told Marvin. "Mrs. Gibbs just arrived." Mrs. Gibbs was president of the PTO.

"The last time she came to school, she checked to see if there was gum in the drinking fountains," Marvin said. "She even inspected the gerbils' cage."

"What if she throws the Armpits out?" Theresa asked.

But there was no opportunity for that. Although Theresa kept running out to the parking lot every five minutes, the Armpits had not appeared.

It was time for the show to begin. Theresa felt her heart sinking.

Stacey came and dragged Theresa up to the stage. "Whether they're here or not, the show's got to go on," she said.

Theresa couldn't help peeking through the curtain for the Armpits. She saw Ms. LaForest in the front row wearing a green velvet jumper that went right down to her ankles.

Theresa's parents were there, too, along with Weird Mom and Stacey's dad, Kevin's parents, the whole Mallow family, the Kewaysaws, Pastor Conway and his wife, and the Ellenbergers, who owned Happy Endings Funeral Home.

"My son, Mark, is the master of cere-monies," Theresa heard Mr. Ellenberger, the funeral director, telling everyone. He was beaming with pride. Usually he was pretty serious.

Mark was wearing one of his father's black suits. It was the oldest of the three black suits Mr. Ellenberger wore for funerals. The trouser legs had been rolled up and the jacket pulled back with clothespins.

Mark made a sweeping bow and announced, "Ladies and gentlemen, it is my pleasure to present a very talented group of performers this evening." There was much applause from the front rows and especially from the fourth grade. "First on the program is Bethany Conway, who will read an original poem."

Bethany was wearing a pink dress with ruffles that had taken Mrs. Conway an hour to iron. Her sash was tied in the back in a butterfly-wing bow. Bethany stood up straight, her arms stiffly at her sides.

Summer Storm

The thunder roars
The gull soars
The raindrops dance
The lightning is a lance
To pierce the tree
And kill me.

Bethany bowed, holding out her pink ruffled dress. She gave the audience a big smile.

There was a pause while everyone looked at each other. Finally Theresa started applauding. Soon the rest of the audience joined in.

Then Mark announced, "And now for the world's fastest feather plucker!"

Marvin Mallow walked onto the stage dragging a dead turkey and a pail of scalding water. The whole Mallow family clapped like crazy. Theresa sighed. There was a little feather in one of Marvin's curls.

Marvin dipped the turkey into the scalding water. After a few minutes, he pulled out the turkey, shook off the water, and started to pull out the loosened feathers. In no time, he was holding up the naked, plucked turkey.

There were cries of "Bravo" from the audience.

Things quieted a little while Baylor Proust gave a very nice talk on "The Diseases of Childhood." Since Baylor always

imagined he had some disease or other, he was especially good at describing how rotten you could feel. He mentioned the sicknesses he'd had and the ones he thought he *might* have had. Baylor talked about rashes and sore throats and earaches and nosebleeds and pains in your side from running.

Mrs. Proust whispered to Mrs. Conway, "I'm sure he'll be a doctor when he grows up."

Kevin gave a talk on all the things you could sue people for.

A man in the audience stood up and shouted, "We'll sue you if you don't bring on the Armpits."

Tommy Kewaysaw strode onto the stage in his buckskin jacket and feathered headdress.

"Aren't some of those turkey feathers?" Theresa whispered.

"Shhh," Bethany said.

Stacey was right behind Tommy. Her hair hung down in two short braids. She wore a sort of Indian dress made out of an old sheet, and carried a set of drums.

At the sound of the drums, Tommy began his dance. There were several Native Americans besides Mr. and Mrs. Kewaysaw in the crowd. They kept time with the drums and called out to encourage Tommy. Tommy went dancing down the stairs. Soon the whole auditorium was stamping and clapping.

Theresa was the last performer. She walked onto the stage and looked nervously at the entrance. There were still no Armpits to be seen. Solemnly Theresa opened her notebook. In a good loud voice, she announced, "I'm going to read a chapter from my novel, *California Sunshine*."

Amber got up late in the morning. Everybody in California gets up when they want to. As usual the sun was shining.

Amber put on her new shorts and T-shirt. She did not make her bed or clean her room. Her parents had three maids. One of the maids had her favorite breakfast all ready for her.

Amber climbed into her red convertible. Although she was only twelve, she could drive. In California anyone who wants to can drive. Amber drove to the ocean. All her friends were sitting in the sun on the beach.

After they went swimming, they had pizza. While they were having pizza, someone in the restaurant was killed by a gangster. When they were finished with their pizza, they solved the murder. Then everyone went back to the beach for the rest of the afternoon.

Trying to kill time, Theresa was about to read the next chapter when the Putrid Armpits walked into the gym. They were carrying their guitars, drums, synthesizers, and amplifiers.

The fans went crazy. Theresa jumped up and down. The members of the school board were frowning. Mr. Chickering looked like he wanted to get up and say something. Maybe *The Pledge of Allegiance.*

Mark hurried Theresa offstage as politely as he could. He cleared his throat about five times.

"Ladies and gentlemen," he said, "I give you the Putrid Armpits."

7
The Armpits Do Their Thing

Lorn, Tech, Spike, and Mitch bounded onto the stage. The Armpits weren't wearing black leather. Their hair wasn't purple.

Mr. Chickering let out a sigh of relief.

There was a pause while the amplifiers and synthesizers were set up. Spike sent for extension cords. Two fuses were blown and replaced.

The president of the school board, Waverly Litcher, turned to Mrs. Gibbs. "As the head of the PTO, Mrs. Gibbs, I wonder if you would say a few words."

Mrs. Gibbs stood up. She looked around nervously and sat back down.

The people in the audience called out requests for their favorite Armpits songs: "Sinking in the Swamp," "Your Spider Eyes," and "My Dull, Dreary, Rotten World."

Backstage, Theresa was desperate. She whispered to Bethany, "If the Armpits start to sing those songs, Mr. Litcher and Mrs. Gibbs might kick them out. Then we'll have to give all the money back."

Theresa and Bethany hurried onstage to explain to the Armpits.

Lorn grabbed the microphone and said, "Excuse me, folks, but we're going to do something a little different tonight. This is the fourth grade's show. They'll pick the tunes. Bethany here suggested a hymn you probably all know, 'Amazing Grace.' I want you to join in."

For a minute, there was a stunned silence. But as the familiar tune came over the amplifier, everyone began to sing. Even Mrs. Gibbs and Mr. Litcher.

"Amazing Grace" was followed by "Someone's in the Kitchen with Dinah," "The Itty Bitty Spider" with hand gestures, and "This Land Is Your Land."

The Armpits' fans began to grumble.

Marvin sidled up to the principal, who was chewing on one of Mrs. Conway's cookies.

"Mr. Chickering, a lot of people paid to hear the Putrid Armpits. Couldn't the band sing just one of their regular songs?" Marvin pleaded.

Mr. Chickering looked very serious and very thoughtful. Actually he wasn't either of those things. He was just enjoying his cookie. Finally the principal of Starvation Lake Elementary threw caution to the wind. "Well, Marvin, just *one.*"

Marvin ran to the stage and gave the Armpits the good word. The amplifiers were turned up. The synthesizers were turned on.

The Armpits asked for requests. The loudest shout of all came from the front row. It was Mrs. Gibbs screaming for the Armpits' hit song, "Don't Throw Up When I Say I Love You."

Mrs. Gibbs looked around her. Her face was beet red. Mr. Litcher's mouth dropped open. Theresa grabbed Stacey's arm. Mrs. Gibbs was an Armpits fan!

The band started the first notes of "Don't Throw Up." Lorn banged on the drums. Spike and Mitch began running

around the stage with their guitars. They were shrieking and shouting.

The Armpits' fans screamed at the top of their voices.

Theresa began to worry as she saw Mr. Litcher take out his pencil. She was sure he wanted to write down the words so he could complain about them later.

After several minutes of blaring sound and rushing around the stage, the music stopped. There was thunderous applause.

Mr. Litcher looked puzzled. With relief Theresa heard him say, "I couldn't understand a word." He put his pencil away.

Mrs. Gibbs hurried toward the exit. Everyone else headed for Mrs. Conway's cookies.

Except Theresa and Marvin, who were counting the money. Theresa could hardly believe it. They had made over three hundred dollars! Serious book money.

❋

On their way home, Theresa and her mother and father drove past Fred's Tire Salvage yard. Her dad was officially on duty, so he was driving his Desolation County Sheriff's car.

He slowed down to greet the firemen. They were still working to put out the remains of the fire. It was an eerie sight. The snow falling out of the night. The smoke curling up into the darkness.

"How long before the fire will be out, Dad?" Theresa asked.

"It'll probably smolder another week, but the worst is over," her dad said.

"They don't have tire fires in California, do they?" Theresa asked.

"Wherever you have tires piled up, it's always a danger," Sheriff Bloncheck said. "Even in California."

But Theresa wasn't listening. She was tired from all the excitement. Lulled by the sound of the engine, she fell asleep. She dreamed the school library was full of books. Each one was a novel and each one had her name on it.

About the Author

Gloria Whelan and her husband live in the woods in northern Michigan about a mile from Starvation Lake. In the real world, it's just a lake. But Gloria used the name for a lake and a town—a town very much like where she lives. "A lot of the characters in this book are children that I wave to in the morning at the bus stops," she says.

The winner of the 1998 Michigan Author of the Year Award, Gloria Whelan is known for historical fiction that captures the past with details of everyday life. Some of her many books include *Once on This Island*, *The Indian School*, and *Homeless Bird*.

If you like *Welcome to Starvation Lake*,
you might also want to read

Ghost Horse
by George Edward Stanley

Emily got out of bed. She ran to the window and pulled back the curtains. In the moonlight, she could see the beautiful white horse!

Emily pinched herself. "Ouch!" Now she knew she wasn't dreaming. The beautiful white horse was really there!

He started walking toward her window. But the closer he got, the paler he got.

Emily gasped. She could see through the horse!

"You're . . . you're a ghost!" she whispered.